Puppy Problem

Lucy Daniels

With special thanks to Sarah Khilam

For Rhea

Illustrations by Jo Anne Davies Artful Doodlers

ORCHARD BOOKS

First published in Great Britain in 2020 by The Watts Publishing Group

1 3 5 7 9 10 8 6 4 2

Text copyright © Working Partners, 2020
Illustrations copyright © Working Partners, 2020

The moral rights of the author and illustrator have been asserted.

A CIP catalogue record for this book
is available from the British Library.

ISBN 978 1 40835 925 9

Printed and bound in Great Britain by Clays Ltd, Elcograf S.p.A

The paper and board used in this book are made from wood from responsible sources.

MIX
Paper from
responsible sources
FSC® C104740

Orchard Books
An imprint of
Hachette Children's Group
Part of The Watts Publishing Group Limited
Carmelite House
50 Victoria Embankment
London EC4Y 0DZ

An Hachette UK Company
www.hachette.co.uk
www.hachettechildrens.co.uk

CONTENTS

CHAPTER ONE

"This driveway goes on for ever!" Amelia Haywood said. It was the last Saturday before the summer half-term and she was walking through the grounds of Brambledown Hall with her mum and her best friend, Sam Baxter. The hall stood in the middle of its own estate,

a large park on the outskirts of Welford
village. There was green grass and trees
as far as she could see. "Do you think
we'll reach the hall before bedtime?
Maybe we'll have to camp out with
the deer!"

"That sounds awesome!" Sam said,
his eyes shining.

Mum laughed, tucking a loose strand
of hair behind her ear. "I'm afraid you
won't need your pyjamas today. We're
nearly there – look!" She pointed at the
beautiful old building ahead.

Amelia grinned. *It's like a fairytale castle!*
It was built of grey stone, with arched
windows and pointed towers in the

corners. She decided to bring a camera with her next time she came, so she could show Dad a photo when she went to visit him in York.

Mum was going to sign up for the annual Welford Gardening Contest. There was going to be a big launch party next weekend, and all the green-fingered villagers were getting ready to show off their gardens. Amelia was more interested in the creatures that lived in the woods around Brambledown Hall, though. *I really hope we see the deer today*, she thought excitedly.

"There!" Sam clutched Amelia's arm.

A cluster of reddish-brown animals grazed a short distance away. A couple of deer lifted their heads to look at them, then turned

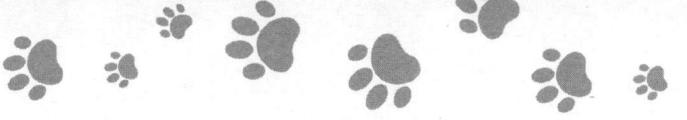

back to nibbling at the grass.

Amelia's heart beat fast. "They're beautiful," she breathed.

A little fawn took a few steps towards them on long, skinny legs. He stumbled and another larger deer nudged him back again.

"Aw," said Amelia, shading her eyes to get a better view. "I wish we could get closer. But I read somewhere that it's not good for wild deer to get used to being around humans."

As they reached the entrance to the hall, Amelia noticed a poster about the Welford Gardening Contest fixed to the door. She read out some of the categories

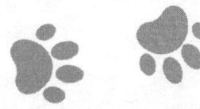

PRETTIEST BORDERS
BEST HEDGES
BIGGEST VEG
RADIANT ROSES

listed below: "Prettiest Borders, Best Hedges, Biggest Veg ... Which one are you entering, Mum?"

"Well, the Biggest Veg contest is definitely out, seeing as slugs ate my cabbages." Mum frowned. "So I think I'm going for the Radiant Roses competition."

"Good idea!" Amelia squeezed Mum's hand. "Your roses are so pretty!"

"Well, let's cross our fingers," Mum said, grinning.

"Just think, Mrs Haywood, if you win, your roses will be on the telly!" said Sam.

For the first time ever, the contest was being filmed for a gardening show called *Blooming Brilliant*. Amelia's gran was a big fan of the presenter, Bernard Bloom – and his pet dog, Pansy.

"Come on," said Amelia. "Let's have a look inside!"

They stepped through the hallway into a big room that was full of tables and chairs, all piled up with pot plants, gardening twine, scissors and trowels. Villagers scurried about, carrying

armfuls of flowers and vegetables. As her mum went to sign up for the Radiant Roses competition, Amelia spotted Julia Kaminski, the receptionist at Animal Ark, sitting in her wheelchair next to a suit of armour. Another woman with long brown hair stood beside her, dressed in a blue hoodie, cutting up strips of ribbon to tie around bouquets. Julia looked up from the flowers she was arranging in a vase and waved at them.

"Hi, Julia!" Sam said.

"Hey there!" Julia replied. "This is my sister, Kasia. She's organising the contest this year." She nudged the woman beside her. "Kasia, this is Amelia and Sam – I

14

told you about them, remember? They're our helpers at Animal Ark!"

Warmth swelled inside Amelia's chest. She was so proud of her role at the vet surgery.

"Lovely to meet you both!" Kasia said. "Isn't this amazing?" She gestured at the

crowd, a smile breaking across her face.

"It's crazy in here!" said Sam. "I suppose everyone wants to win and get on TV."

"Is Bernard Bloom here yet?" Amelia asked, hopefully. "My gran would love it if I could get his autograph for her."

"I'm afraid we've only got his picture so far." Kasia pointed to a cardboard cut-out behind her. It showed a man with twinkling blue eyes and floppy blond hair. He was holding Pansy, a Jack Russell cross terrier

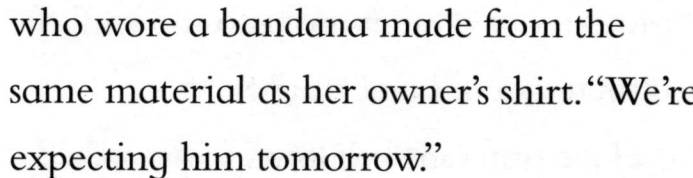

who wore a bandana made from the same material as her owner's shirt. "We're expecting him tomorrow."

"He's going to be staying at our Bed and Breakfast," Sam told her proudly.

"Kasia, tell Amelia and Sam about Blossom!" Julia said, tying a red ribbon around her flowers.

Kasia grinned. "Blossom's my new Cockapoo puppy. Would you like to meet her?"

"Yes, please!" Amelia's heart raced — she loved meeting new animals! *I've never seen a Cockapoo before,* she thought. *I wonder what it will look like?*

Kasia turned towards a closed door.

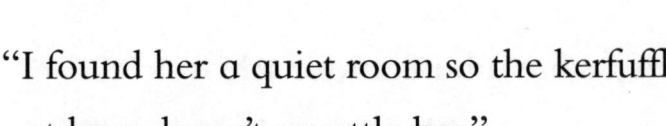

"I found her a quiet room so the kerfuffle out here doesn't unsettle her."

"Have you had her long?" Sam asked.

"Only a few days," Kasia said. "In her last home, the cat kept chasing her out of the house. She hid in the recycling box once and nearly got collected by the bin men!"

"You know, we could help train her," Amelia offered hopefully.

"We trained my Westie, Mac," added Sam. "And he was a real handful! Actually, he still is."

Kasia laughed. "That's very kind of you. But Blossom's already trained! In fact, her last owner crate-trained her."

She opened the door for them.

Amelia was about to ask what crate-training was, but she was distracted by the empty room. There was no sign of a puppy anywhere.

"Um, where is she?" Sam asked.

Kasia dashed in after them and gasped. "Blossom's gone!" She looked around desperately. She darted over to the windows, checking they were all shut.

Worry spiked through Amelia's stomach. Where *had* Blossom gone?

Then she noticed a soft rumbling sound coming from a flowerpot in the corner. Amelia peered inside. She made out a pair of ears and a cute quivering

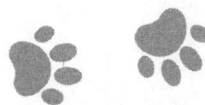

nose amongst the bundle of curly black and white fur squeezed into the bottom of the pot. "Here she is!" she called. She lifted the warm, sleepy little puppy out.

"Thank goodness!" Kasia gasped. She took Blossom and cuddled her close, kissing her head. "You might be called Blossom, but that doesn't mean I can plant you in a pot and grow you!"

Blossom gave Kasia a sleepy lick on the nose.

Kasia giggled. "Thanks, Amelia."

Amelia looked back at the bustling hall and felt a squirm of anxiety. Kasia had adopted a puppy at a really busy time. Would Blossom need help to settle into Welford?

Blossom's already been trained, Amelia reasoned. *She should be fine ... shouldn't she?*

CHAPTER TWO

Cockapoos are a mix of Cocker Spaniel and Poodle, Amelia read. It was Monday evening and she was curled up on the sofa, looking at an animal website on her tablet. *They're loving and energetic, but they can easily get bored.* She scrolled through some photos, stopping to smile at a

picture of a Cockapoo puppy nestled amongst a pile of cuddly toys. He was much cuter than the stuffed animals around him!

She glanced up at the clock. She had ten minutes before she needed to head down to Animal Ark to help at the surgery. Turning back to her tablet, she looked up crate-training. *Puppies are encouraged to sleep and relax in a cage-like box called a crate. They can be placed in these overnight, or when their owner is out.*

Hearing a cry in the back garden, she sat bolt upright. "Are you OK, Mum?" she shouted.

She dashed outside and found Mum in

front of her flower border, her shoulders slumped. "What's wrong?" Amelia asked.

"Something's had a go at my roses." Mum waved at the bushes that grew along the fence. "They're not exactly radiant any more!"

Amelia looked at the bushes and her heart sank. Roses drooped from the branches. Several flowers had hardly

any petals left. "Maybe it was the slugs again?" Amelia suggested. She bit her lip. *Poor Mum.* She'd been so excited about showing off her flowers to Bernard Bloom.

Mum sighed. "There's a few left untouched near the top. I can still put a decent bouquet together. But I don't want the culprit to come back and finish those off too!"

Amelia glanced at the tablet still in her hand. The time on the screen read 5:40. "I'd better go. But you can borrow this – I bet there's some advice online about how to make slugs go away."

"Thanks," Mum said, taking the tablet

and giving Amelia a quick hug. "Have a good time at the surgery."

As Amelia left through the front garden, she noticed the soil was dry. It hadn't rained for days. Could slugs really be to blame for eating Mum's roses? *But if slugs didn't eat them, then who did?*

When Amelia turned into the driveway at Animal Ark, she spotted a dark-haired man crouched down in the flowerbed, digging with a trowel.

"Mr Hope?" she asked, uncertainly.

He turned around, his glasses sitting skewed on his nose, and smiled. "Hello,

 Amelia!" He craned his neck a little and then raised his trowel in a wave. "Hello, Sam and Mac!"

Amelia glanced back and saw them running down the driveway behind her.

"Guess who just arrived at the B&B?" Sam said breathlessly. "Bernard Bloom! I helped Dad to check him in – and his dog, too!"

"Does he look the same as on TV?" Amelia asked.

"Yes, only much hairier!" Sam blinked. "Oh, wait – I thought you meant the dog!" He giggled.

"I heard Mr Bloom likes to stay locally when he films," Mr Hope said, standing up and brushing soil from his knees. "He scouts out the best spots for filming himself. That's why I'm digging." He pointed at several boxes of pansies waiting to be planted. "I'm entering the Prettiest Border competition. Hopefully Mr Bloom will like it so much, he'll do some filming here!"

Amelia squinted at the scooped-out shapes in the soil. "What design are you making?" she asked.

Mr Hope blushed. "It's meant to be a pawprint made from pansies. It's in honour of Pansy!"

"Can we help?" asked Sam, grinning.

Amelia nodded. It looked like fun. *And Mr Hope's outline will need a bit more work to look like a pawprint!*

"That would be great!" Mr Hope peered at the instructions on the pansy boxes. "We need to dig a hole for each

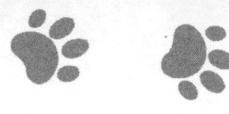

plant, deep enough to protect the roots. Like this, I suppose …" He scooped out some more soil and placed a plant inside the hole.

"No, Mac!" Sam shouted as his puppy tried to dig up the plant Mr Hope had just bedded into the soil. He picked Mac up and lifted him away.

"Hey, how's it going?" Julia came out of the surgery and wheeled her chair towards them, Blossom trotting along beside her.

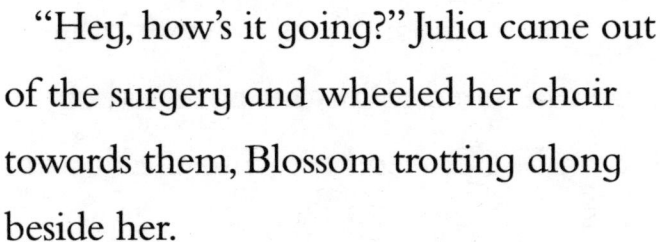

"Hello, Blossom!" Amelia said, as the puppy ran over to her, ears flopping. She ruffled the white fur on Blossom's tummy. "Do you work here now too?"

"I should train her to answer the phone!" Julia laughed. "Kasia is working overtime today, so I'm keeping an eye on Blossom for her."

Mac sniffed at Blossom, and she sniffed  back. Both dogs yapped and chased each other around in circles. Blossom pounced at Mac and he darted back into the flower bed.

"Blossom! That's enough!" Julia called out. "Kasia won't be happy if she has to give you a bath when she gets home from work!"

"You too, Mac!" Sam shouted. "Come out of there!"

Blossom trotted neatly back to Julia. But Mac kept scampering across the soil, nosing at the holes Mr Hope had dug.

"Come on!" Sam pulled Mac away, clipping the lead on. He glanced at Blossom, who was now trotting back towards the surgery behind Julia. "Wow. Blossom's so well trained ... let's hope her good behaviour rubs off on Mac a bit!"

Amelia remembered what Kasia had said about Blossom being crate-trained. She knelt down beside Mr Hope and handed him a plant from one of the boxes. "Do you know anything about

crate-training?" she asked.

Mr Hope took the pansy and positioned it in the soil. "Well, it's quite common in some countries and getting more popular here." He sprinkled compost around the plant's roots. "Some people swear it's the best way to house-train a dog."

Amelia watched Blossom follow Julia into the surgery, her tail wagging. *Blossom looks really happy*, she thought. *She's going to love living in Welford!*

CHAPTER THREE

"Did you pack your toothbrush?" Gran
asked on Tuesday evening.

"Yes, Gran. And my pyjamas!" Amelia
replied, tying up her trainer laces.

"I baked some cookies for you and
Sam." Gran tucked a small tub into
Amelia's rucksack. "And if you should

happen to see Bernard Bloom …"

"I'll get his autograph for you!" Amelia grinned as she pecked Gran on the cheek and headed out the door. Gran had been so excited when she'd heard that Amelia was going to the B&B for a sleepover. Amelia was excited too, and she burst into a sprint down her street and out on to the main road.

A few minutes later, just as she was about to turn up the B&B's front path, she saw Kasia and Blossom walking towards her. "Hello!" she called out.

"Evening, Amelia!" Kasia said. "Although it's more like morning for me. I'm working the night shift, you see.

I just need to
settle Blossom
down and
then I'll head
off."

"Where
do you work?" Amelia asked, crouching
down to stroke Blossom. The puppy
rolled on to her back and gave a happy
sigh as Amelia rubbed her tummy.

"At Walton Hospital," Kasia said. "I'm
a doctor."

"Oh, cool!" Before she came to
Welford, Amelia had wanted to be a
doctor. She'd loved the idea of helping
people get better. But now she wanted

to be a vet and help animals get better instead!

"This is the first night shift I've done since I adopted Blossom, so I hope she won't be too confused," said Kasia.

Blossom licked Amelia's fingers, making her laugh. *She'll be on her own tonight!* Amelia realised. She stood up again, worry knotting her stomach. "Has Blossom got lots of toys to play with? I read on my tablet that Cockapoos get bored easily … Oh!" Her cheeks burned. "Sorry, you probably know that already. I didn't mean to be bossy!"

"It's no problem!" Kasia gave Amelia's shoulder a quick squeeze. "And don't worry about Blossom. She's got the whole of downstairs to tear around in and plenty of toys to keep her entertained while I'm out!"

Amelia smiled with relief. "Sounds like you'll have fun!" she told Blossom.

"I'd better get on," Kasia said, crossing the road and heading towards a house on the other side. It had a tidy lawn and pretty flowerbeds at the front. "Bye, Amelia – nice to see you again!"

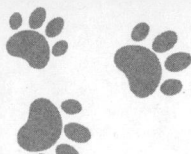
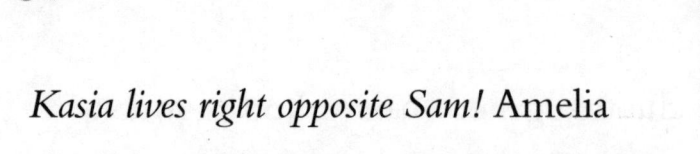

Kasia lives right opposite Sam! Amelia realised happily, turning down the B&B's path. *We'll get to see Blossom all the time!*

Sam answered the door holding a bowl of popcorn. "Mum's set up the DVD player in my room. We're going to watch *101 Dalmatians* – have you seen it?"

"Only a hundred times!" Amelia laughed.

"Then let's make it a hundred and one!" said Sam, grinning.

Amelia dreamed she was surrounded by lots of spotty dogs, all barking at her because they wanted her autograph.

40

Suddenly she was awake. Or was she? She wasn't in her own bed and she could still hear barking.

From the streetlight seeping through a gap in the curtains, Amelia spied a poster of a Westie puppy on the wall. Blinking, she remembered that she was having a sleepover at Sam's house. *That must be Mac barking …*

"Shush, Mac," Sam said sleepily from the other side of the room. "You'll wake everyone up!"

"Uh oh!" Amelia winced, hearing creaking floorboards and grumbling voices in the neighbouring rooms.

Sam's bedroom door opened and light

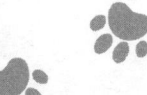

flooded in from the outside landing. Amelia saw Mac barking in his basket before Sam ran over and picked him up.

"What's up with Mac?" Mrs Baxter asked, coming into the room. Mr Baxter followed her in, yawning.

"I don't know," said Sam, stroking Mac who had stopped barking now and was trying to lick his hand instead.

"He's not usually like this at night," said Mrs Baxter, frowning. "Maybe he heard something downstairs?"

"I'll take a look," Mr Baxter said. "Stay here."

An animal's howl came from outside and everyone looked at the window.

Amelia drew the curtain back and peered out. The pavement outside was empty, but she could still hear howling. She stared at the house across the road. The curtains were open but there were no lights on inside. "It must be Blossom!" she cried. "She's on her own over there

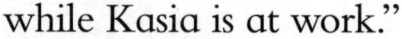

while Kasia is at work."

"That's probably why Mac was barking," said Sam. "He could hear her." He grabbed his hoodie and pulled it on. "We have to check on Blossom – she could be hurt! Can we go over, Dad?"

Mr Baxter hesitated, then nodded. "OK, but I'll come with you."

"I'll phone Kasia and let her know what's happening," said Mrs Baxter. "She texted me earlier about the gardening contest, so I've got her number."

As Amelia and Sam put their trainers on in the hall, Mac wagged his tail expectantly, hoping for a night-time walk. Mrs Baxter picked him up. "I'd

44

better find a treat to
keep you quiet," she said,
carrying him towards the
kitchen.

"What's all that noise?"
Mr Ferguson, a regular
guest at the B&B, called
out from the landing.
"It's not that pesky dog again, is it?"

"My dog?" A man with floppy blond
hair walked out on to the landing,
clutching a yapping Jack Russell terrier.
He was dressed in flowery pyjamas,
and the dog had a matching flowery
bandana round her neck. "There, there,
Pansy," the man said, stroking the

barking dog.

That's Bernard Bloom! Amelia thought excitedly. *Now is probably not the best time to ask for his autograph though …*

"Oh, no, Mr Bloom! Your dog is very well-behaved!" Mr Ferguson said hastily, his face reddening.

"There's another dog barking over the road," Mr Baxter explained to the guests. "It set these two off. I'm so sorry – we'll calm it down, so you can all go back to sleep again."

The cool night air hit Amelia's cheeks as she left the B&B with Sam and his dad. There was a faint orange glow on the horizon. *Is that the sunrise?* She glanced at her watch and read 5:04. *It's almost morning!*

As they walked up Kasia's garden path, Blossom's barking became louder. "She's got a strong pair of lungs for a little puppy!" Amelia said.

"She's waking up the neighbours!" Sam whispered. Several lights were on in nearby houses and people were leaning out of windows to see where the noise was coming from.

"Blossom sounds scared," Amelia said.

She opened Kasia's letterbox and peered through. *I hope she's OK …*

CHAPTER FOUR

At first, Amelia couldn't see anything
at all. But as her eyes got used to the
darkness, she made out a staircase on one
side of the large downstairs room and a
sofa in the middle. She couldn't see any
other furniture, though, and there was no
sign of Blossom.

But she could still hear howling and it tore at her heartstrings. "Blossom! Are you OK?" Amelia called through the letterbox.

The howling stopped and Amelia heard the skitter of claws against the

floorboards. Suddenly the Cockapoo was on the other side of the door, staring up at Amelia, big-eyed.

"You're all right!" Amelia let out a huge

breath, relief flooding through her.

Blossom blinked and was quiet for a moment. Then she howled again and started to dash from one side of the room to the other.

"She doesn't look hurt, but she's really upset," Amelia said, as the puppy raced from wall to wall.

"Maybe she's scared of the dark?" Sam suggested. "Dad, you've got that little torch on your keyring, haven't you? Let's try using it to give Blossom some light."

Mr Baxter unclipped the torch keyring and pressed it into Amelia's palm. She pushed the switch and shone the beam through the letterbox.

Blossom paused and looked around. *It worked! Thank goodness!* But then she started howling again. Amelia's heart dropped into her stomach. *Oh no …*

"Haven't you sorted that dog out yet?" Amelia heard the clomp of heavy boots and turned to see Mr Ferguson striding towards them. "I've got an important meeting in the morning and now I haven't had enough sleep." Mr Ferguson stayed at the B&B when he was working in Welford.

"What is that racket?" complained a woman marching up the garden path, wearing slippers and a dressing gown. More people crowded behind her, all

grumbling.

Amelia, Sam and
Mr Baxter looked
at each other
helplessly.

"I'll try and
calm her down,"
Sam said, not
looking confident. He called through the
letterbox. "Hey, Blossom! What's up?"
But Blossom carried on howling.

"Blossom! What's wrong?" Kasia's voice
rang out as she pushed her way through
the crowd, frowning anxiously. She was
still wearing green hospital scrubs, with
her coat draped over her arm.

Kasia unlocked her door and ran inside, throwing her coat on the floor. "What's wrong?" she repeated, stroking Blossom. The puppy promptly stopped howling, licked Kasia's hand, then crept under the hood of her coat, her paws and nose just visible.

"She seems fine now," Kasia said, looking very confused.

"I suppose she can smell you on your coat," Amelia said. "Maybe it's comforting?"

Kasia turned to the crowd outside. "I'm so

sorry, everyone. It won't happen again – I promise!"

People started to drift away, still grumbling, and Kasia switched on the lights. Amelia's eyes widened – the room was massive! The walls were painted white, and the few pieces of furniture were sleek and silver, with black leather cushions.

Sam nudged her. "There's so much space. Mac would love dashing around in here!" he whispered.

"Is Blossom usually a noisy puppy?" Mr Baxter asked his neighbour.

Kasia's forehead wrinkled. "Not at all," she said. "She's usually quite quiet and she was fast asleep when I left for work. I don't know what's set her off but I hope it doesn't happen again … I'm working nights all week!"

Gentle snores came from under the coat on the floor. "Look!" Amelia pointed. "She's completely worn out after all that rushing around! What if me and Sam take her out on a long walk tomorrow evening? Then she might sleep all through the night."

"That would be great!" Kasia said. "Thank you!"

Amelia's heart swelled with excitement. *If we can't tire Blossom out, no one can!*

The next evening, Amelia and Sam led
Blossom and Mac all around Welford
and through the surrounding fields. They
climbed over a stile and crossed the road,
heading over to the wildlife sanctuary
that Amelia and Sam had created not
long ago.

They let Blossom and Mac off their
leads, and the puppies tore off into the
long grass. Blossom darted behind a log.
She was very quiet, but Mac tracked her
down and chased her back out. Mac
ducked under a bush, but he was so
excited about his hiding place that he
couldn't stop barking and Blossom found
him straight away.

"They're playing hide and seek!"
Amelia said, grinning.

"Mac's not very good at it, though!"
Sam said. His eyes lit up. "Oh, is that a
chaffinch?" He pointed at a bird with a
blue head and red chest, pecking at the
ground beneath a bush.

"That's the first one I've seen here!" Amelia said excitedly. "We can add it to the signs we made!"

Mac bounded towards them, barking, and the 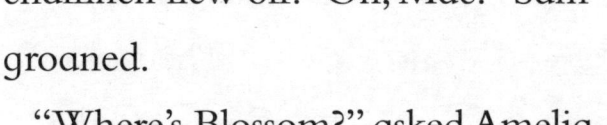 chaffinch flew off. "Oh, Mac!" Sam groaned.

"Where's Blossom?" asked Amelia, looking around. "She's hidden herself a bit too well!"

"We don't want her falling asleep out here," Sam said, frowning. "She needs to save that sleepiness for tonight."

Where would I hide if I was a puppy?
Amelia wondered. She caught sight of a
hollow tree, and, sure enough, there was
Blossom, curled up inside. The puppy
looked up at Amelia with a little twinkle
in her eye. Amelia smiled. *She looks a lot*

*happier now
than she did
last night!*

They set off
home. Along
the way,
they passed
a house with
several people

gathered around a bush in the front garden, their voices raised. Amelia recognised a slightly older girl with long black hair. "Look – there's Charlene Girtz."

Sam nodded. "And her family. What's going on?"

Charlene looked up and waved. "Have you got a new dog, Amelia? She's cute!"

"She's not mine, I'm just walking her," Amelia explained. "Is everything OK?"

Charlene's face fell. "It's our roses. We were going to enter them in the Radiant Roses competition, but someone's pulled the heads off."

Amelia gasped as she saw the damaged

flowers. "The same thing happened to my mum's roses!" she said. A thought struck her and she felt slightly worried. "You don't think someone's wrecking other people's roses so they can win the contest, do you?"

Sam frowned. "Who would do that?"

"Tiffany Banks said she was sure her father's roses would win the competition!" said Charlene.

Amelia and Sam's classmate Tiffany liked to show off. "But Tiffany wouldn't do anything that mean ... would she?" said Amelia.

"We'd better warn anyone else we  know who is entering the competition to

keep their eyes open," Charlene said.

Amelia nodded. "Good thinking. We need to get Blossom home now. We'll see you at the launch party on Saturday!"

When Kasia opened her front door a short while later, she was already wearing her coat. "Thanks so much!" she said, tying her hair up in a clip. "Blossom looks exhausted!" As if to prove Kasia's point, the puppy ran over to a bag on the bottom stair, jumped inside and instantly fell asleep.

"Hey, I need that for work!" Kasia

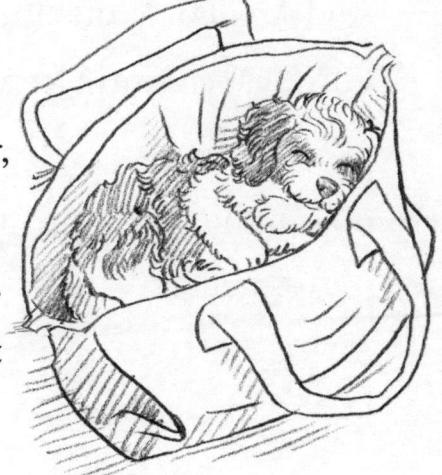

said, laughing. She lifted Blossom out of the bag, still snoozing, and placed her on the sofa. "There, that's better!"

As Amelia and Sam headed home, Mac shuffled along behind them. "He's so tired, he can't even be bothered to wag his tail!" laughed Sam, scooping his puppy up.

"Looks like it's mission accomplished," said Amelia, scratching Mac behind the ears. "Operation Sleepy Pup is a success!"

CHAPTER FIVE

"Morning!" Sam poked his head out of the B&B dining room window and waved at Amelia as she walked up the front path. She hadn't been able to resist dropping in before school to find out what had happened. Sam ducked back inside and opened the front door before

she had even reached it, his eyes shining.

"Did it work? Was Blossom quiet?" asked Amelia, following him into the house.

Sam grinned. "Yep! I slept all through the night!"

"Phew! Well done, Blossom!" Amelia clapped her hands.

Footsteps on the stairs made them look up. Bernard Bloom trudged down, rubbing his eyes. Pansy trotted behind him in a pink dog coat that perfectly matched Bernard's sweater.

Mrs Baxter rushed out of the kitchen clutching a basket filled with fruit. A pair of earplugs lay on top. She pressed the

basket into Mr Bloom's hands. "We're so sorry about the noise last night. Please accept this with our apologies!"

Amelia bit her lip. It didn't sound as though the night had gone as well as Sam had thought!

Mr Bloom stared down at the basket

and then back up at Mrs Baxter. "It's not your fault, but thanks anyway," he said, shuffling into the dining room wearily.

"Was Blossom howling again?" Amelia asked Mrs Baxter.

Sam's mum nodded, stifling a yawn. "All night! And I couldn't get hold of Kasia this time. Thankfully, we're the only B&B around here that allows pets, or I think Bernard Bloom would have checked out by now!" She turned back into the kitchen, shaking her head.

Amelia looked over at Sam and raised her eyebrows.

Sam rubbed his nose, looking sheepish. "I must have been so tired from our walk

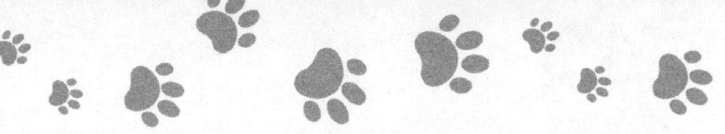

that I slept through it all!"

Amelia's forehead tightened. "Poor Blossom must be exhausted. We should check on her, in case Kasia isn't back from work yet …"

As they ran up Kasia's garden path, Amelia noticed the front door was wide open. "Hello!" she called out, peering into the house. She saw Kasia standing by the far window, wiping her eyes with her coat sleeve. Kasia looked up and beckoned them in.

Amelia stepped inside and stared in astonishment. Shredded posters littered the floor. Compost bags had been ripped open and soil was scattered everywhere.

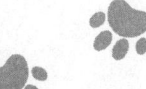

"What happened?" Amelia asked.

"This is all stuff I was storing for the gardening contest ..." Kasia waved at the mess strewn about.

"Where's Blossom?" Amelia asked.

Kasia pointed at the corner of the room where Blossom crouched, her fur smudged with soil. She held up a paw and a drop of blood fell on to the floor. "Uh oh!" gasped Amelia. "She's hurt!"

"Oh no!" Kasia paled. She pulled a compost bag aside and Amelia saw a pile of broken glass. "Oh gosh, that was the winner's trophy!" Kasia cried. "She must have cut herself on the glass! I need to get her to the vet!"

While Kasia ran upstairs to fetch a blanket, Sam and Amelia crouched down beside Blossom. "I don't understand," said Sam, frowning.

"She got loads of exercise yesterday. So why was she still barking and running around?"

"I suppose if she couldn't sleep, she must have got really agitated." Amelia stroked Blossom's back. "You poor thing," she said softly. "I wish we knew what's upsetting you. We might be able to help!"

"That's weird," said Sam, as they walked up Animal Ark's driveway. "The pawprint picture is all scuffed up!" He pointed at the flowerbed where Mr Hope had planted pansies for the gardening competition. Many of them had lost their petals, and some plants had no flowers left on them at all.

"I wonder if it's the same person who wrecked the roses?" said Amelia. "Maybe it's not just about winning the Radiant Roses competition. Perhaps they're trying to ruin *all* the competitions!"

"Don't say that!" Kasia said, looking alarmed. "I can't cope with anything else going wrong …"

They went into the surgery. In the examination room, Mrs Hope cleaned Blossom's paw and checked there was no glass caught in the wound, while Kasia explained what had happened. "I just don't understand," she said. "There's plenty of space in the house for her to play. I leave her with food, water and

toys. I don't know what else I can do for her!"

Mrs Hope looked thoughtful as she started bandaging Blossom's paw. "I think she might be experiencing isolation distress. Some dogs really don't like to be alone."

"That could be it. Poor Blossom ..." Kasia's voice trembled. "But I often have to work nights. I tried to find a dog-sitter for her, but all the ones around here only take dogs in the daytime."

Amelia's heart thumped as an idea struck her. "Maybe I could look after Blossom at night? She can stay with me and … oh no!" Amelia's face fell as she remembered her kitten and instantly saw the flaw in her plan. "Star definitely won't like sharing her house with a strange dog!"

"My house would be OK, though," said Sam. "Mac would love it if Blossom came for a sleepover. And if it means we all have a quiet night, Mum and Dad definitely won't mind! Let's try it tonight. You can stay over too, Amelia! It's half-term tomorrow, after all."

"Awesome!" Amelia nodded

enthusiastically. "I just need to check with Mum and Gran."

"That would be amazing, Sam," Kasia said, looking relieved. "Thank you so much."

Whilst Mrs Hope finished bandaging Blossom, Sam popped out to phone his parents from reception. He returned a couple of minutes later and gave a thumbs up, smiling.

"Blossom's good to go now," said Mrs Hope, taking the stained cotton swabs over to the bin. "But she shouldn't put too much weight on that paw for the next couple of days."

Amelia reached out to stroke the

puppy. "No more running around the wilderness for a while! We'll have a brilliant time tonight though." She smiled as Blossom licked her fingers. *And hopefully I can get Bernard Bloom's autograph for Gran!*

"Come on," said Sam. "We'd better hurry or we'll be late for school."

CHAPTER SIX

"Wow, this room is fancy!" exclaimed
Amelia, looking around the bedroom
they were staying in for their sleepover.
It was much bigger than Sam's bedroom.
It had two double beds, and a chandelier
hung from the high ceiling. She placed
her overnight bag on one of the beds.

"It's the biggest room in the house," said Sam, dropping an armful of Mac's toys on to the floor. "Bernard Bloom was in here to start with. But he said it was too draughty so Mum moved him into a smaller room." He grinned. "There's loads of space for the puppies to play if they wake up in the night!"

Mac tried to nudge Blossom into a chasing game, but she pressed against Amelia, her tail between her legs.

"Sorry, Mac," said Amelia, scooping the Cockapoo up. "Blossom can't run around too

much. She needs to mind her paw."

Mrs Baxter came in, carrying the puppies' baskets. "I really hope this works!" she said, putting the baskets on the floor. "Someone else checked out this morning because of Blossom's barking. At this rate, we won't have any guests left!"

"She's been really quiet since she hurt her paw," Amelia said, placing Blossom in her basket. "I think she'll sleep well tonight." Amelia hoped she sounded more confident than she felt. And as she settled into bed, she crossed her fingers for luck …

When Amelia woke up the next morning, she could hear pans clattering in the kitchen downstairs and a radio playing in the next room. But no dog barking!

"It worked! The puppies slept through the night!" Amelia bounded out of bed to give Blossom a congratulatory cuddle.

Mac was still fast asleep in his basket, snoring gently. But Blossom's basket was empty!

"Blossom's missing!" Amelia's heart pounded as she woke Sam up. "We have to find her!"

They searched under the beds and behind the armchair, but there was no

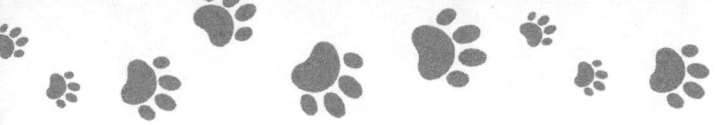

sign of the puppy. "She must have got out of the room!" Sam said, heading out on to the landing. His mum was polishing the banister rail and Sam quickly explained that Blossom was missing.

"I'll search downstairs," Mrs Baxter said, looking worried. "You check the rooms up here. Just the empty ones, though – don't disturb the guests!"

Sam led Amelia along the landing. "That's Bernard Bloom's room," he whispered as they passed the first closed door. "This one's empty, though …" He pushed at a door that was slightly ajar and Amelia followed him into a

small room with a single bed.

A funny noise was coming from an open drawer in the bedside table. *That sounds just like snoring …*

"There she is!" said Amelia, peering into the drawer. Blossom was curled up inside, fast asleep!

"Phew! I'll let Mum know …" Sam left the room and his footsteps clattered down the stairs.

 Amelia watched Blossom's chest move up and down as she slept peacefully. She

frowned. If Blossom had been barking because she didn't like to be apart from people, why had she taken herself off to an empty room?

As Blossom twitched her nose and sighed, Amelia smiled. *She must be having a lovely dream!* The puppy looked so cute, curled up in the drawer.

She does seem to like hiding in small spaces, Amelia thought, remembering how Blossom had curled up inside the flower pot … and inside the hollow tree … and inside Kasia's bag …

"Oh!" Amelia sat down on the bed, her hand pressed against her mouth. What had she read on her tablet about crate-training? *The puppy sleeps and relaxes in a cage-like box.* Was it possible that Blossom had got so used to small spaces, that those were the only places where she felt comfortable?

"Kasia's house doesn't have any hiding places, does it, Blossom?" Amelia whispered, her heart beating fast. "It's not human company you're desperate for. You want to be in a little den!"

When Sam returned, Amelia explained her theory.

His eyes lit up, and he nodded. "It makes sense. We should go online and see if any other crate-trained dogs prefer small spaces." He frowned. "Mum's using

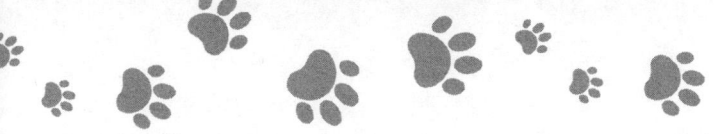

the computer right now, though."

"Kasia doesn't finish work for another hour," said Amelia. "Let's go to my house and look it up on my tablet. We can drop Blossom off on our way back."

Once she was washed and dressed, Amelia reached into the drawer and lifted Blossom out. The puppy snuggled into Amelia's arms, burying her face in her hoodie. "You can keep on snoozing," Amelia said. "I'll carry you, so you don't put too much weight on that paw."

"Can you go in and make sure Star is out of the way?" Amelia asked Sam, once

they had arrived at her house. "If Gran's around, maybe she can distract her?"

Sam ran back out a minute later. "It's OK, your gran's giving Star cuddles – I'm not sure who's enjoying it more!"

Amelia went through to the living room and put Blossom on the carpet, so she could switch her tablet on. But at once Blossom bolted through the back door, barking loudly.

"Blossom! Stop!" Amelia chased after her, her heart pounding. "You'll hurt your paw!"

Sam rushed out into the garden behind her. He grabbed her arm as they both came to a sudden stop. "What on earth ..." he gasped.

A deer!

It stood over a rose bush, pink petals falling from its mouth. Seeing Amelia and Sam, it took several steps back, its reddish-brown coat gleaming in the morning light.

Amelia and Sam glanced at each other. Sam's mouth hung open in astonishment.

Amelia drew a sharp breath. "Is that the flower vandal?"

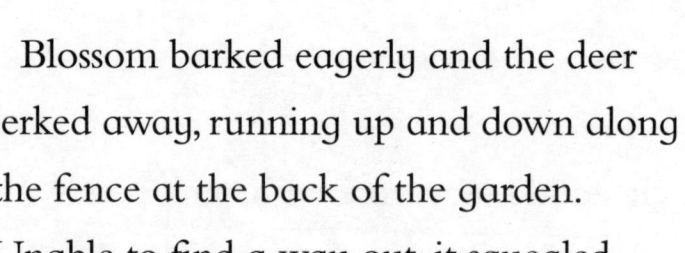

Blossom barked eagerly and the deer jerked away, running up and down along the fence at the back of the garden. Unable to find a way out, it squealed in anguish. *Oh, the poor thing!* thought Amelia, her stomach knotting with worry. *It's completely terrified!*

CHAPTER SEVEN

The deer ran straight at Amelia. For a
moment, she couldn't move. Her legs
were frozen in shock.

"Watch out!" yelled Sam.

Amelia threw herself sideways and the
deer lurched away, its eyes flashing, and
sprang towards the fence instead. *Please*

jump over! Amelia thought desperately. But Blossom barked, and the deer stumbled to the side.

"Blossom's making things worse!" Amelia cried out. "The deer's going to hurt itself!" She crouched down, trying to catch Blossom, but the puppy dodged around her hands and charged towards the deer.

Sam leapt in front of Blossom. The puppy tried to circle around him but now Amelia ran in front of her, forcing Blossom even further away from the deer. Working together, Amelia and Sam herded Blossom towards the kitchen door and chased her inside. They ran in after her and slammed the door shut.

Gran and Mum rushed downstairs. "What's going on?" asked Mum. "We heard a shrieking noise!'

"A deer got into the garden – look!" Amelia pointed at the window. The poor deer was bounding towards the fence, as if it was about to vault over it. But at the last minute it veered away. It careered around the garden, desperately searching

for a way out.

"How did it get in?" Sam said, picking up Blossom and stroking her. "Your garden has a fence around it."

"Deer can easily jump over two-metre fences," said Gran.

"But it's panicking," Mum pointed out. "That must be why it's not jumping out again."

"How are we going to help it escape?" Amelia bit her lip, worry building up inside her. The deer stopped running and looked all around wildly, its chest moving in and out as it gasped for breath.

"We could try lifting one of the fence panels up," suggested Gran.

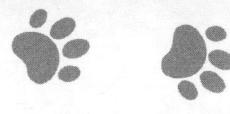

"Won't it get stuck in someone else's garden?" Sam asked, still stroking Blossom.

Gran shook her head. "The grass on the other side of the fence leads into the woodland behind Brambledown Hall. Once it's out of the garden, I expect it'll find its way back to its herd."

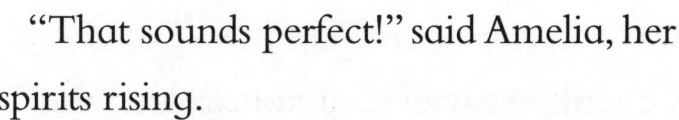

"That sounds perfect!" said Amelia, her spirits rising.

"We'd better move the panel from the other side of the fence, so we don't scare the deer any more than we have already," Mum said, heading out into the hallway. She got a stepladder out from the cupboard at the bottom of the stairs.

Gran opened the front door and helped Mum carry it outside.

"I'll stay inside and keep an eye on Blossom," Sam said, as the puppy tried to wriggle out of his arms. "Or she'll tear around the house and hurt her paw."

"Oh yes – and please make sure she doesn't scare Star," Amelia added.

Amelia, Gran and Mum walked along the path between their cottage and the house next door, coming out behind their garden. Gran set up the stepladder. "Right, Amelia, you're our eyes!" she said. "If you climb up and watch the deer, you can warn us if it comes near while we're moving the panel."

While Gran and Mum started to ease
a fence panel up between its concrete
posts, Amelia climbed the stepladder
and peered over. The deer had stopped
running and was looking curiously at
the fence.

"Nearly there!" Mum gasped as she
and Gran lifted the panel higher.

The deer broke into a run towards the
widening gap.

"It's coming!" Amelia cried.

The deer thudded across the grass. Amelia felt the air rush against her cheeks as it flew through the gap below the fence panel and bolted into the trees behind them.

"Phew!" Amelia let out a big gasp of relief as the sound of pounding hooves faded in the woods. She climbed down from the stepladder and helped Mum and Gran lower the fence panel into place again.

Back in the kitchen, Sam was sitting on the floor, looking at Amelia's tablet. Blossom was curled up inside the laundry basket beside him, nestled in a heap of clean clothes.

"I've been reading about crate-training," he said, pointing at Amelia's tablet. "I think you're right about Blossom needing small spaces." He looked down at the laundry basket. "We'd better let Kasia know what we've discovered …"

A little later, Amelia and Sam walked up Kasia's garden path. Amelia held  Blossom and, as she reached out to press the doorbell, Blossom licked her nose, making her giggle. Mac sat on the doormat in front of them, wagging his little tail.

When Kasia opened the door, she smiled widely. And then she looked down at the laundry basket Sam was holding, full of blankets.

"Is it wash day?" she asked, her forehead creasing.

"We've got something to show you!" Amelia said, handing Blossom over to her.

Kasia stood back to let them in, looking amused. Sam placed the basket on the floor, and Amelia dragged a pair

of dining chairs over, positioning a chair
on either side of the basket. Sam draped
a large blanket across the backs of the
chairs so it hung over the laundry basket,
and Amelia plumped up the blankets
inside.

"It's a little den!" Amelia said as she
stood up. She took Blossom back from
Kasia, carried her over to the basket and
placed her inside. Blossom turned in a

circle, curling herself up into a tight ball.

"We think that her crate-training means Blossom feels safest in small spaces," Amelia explained. "So this room seems really big and scary to her, as there's nowhere to curl up inside. We noticed that she liked the flowerpot at Brambledown Hall, and your handbag. And last night she slept in a little drawer at Sam's house."

Kasia stared at the den for a moment, then clapped her hands. "You could be right! And actually, a den is better than a crate because she can come and go as she wants!"

"I don't think she's going anywhere

right now," said Sam. "And, fingers crossed, she'll settle down tonight."

"I hope so!" Kasia replied. "It's the launch of the gardening contest tomorrow. I could use a good night's sleep. Actually, I could do with a cosy den just like Blossom's to curl up in!"

As they left Kasia's house, Amelia crossed her fingers tight. *I hope the den works*, she thought. *I don't think anyone will stand for another night of barking!*

CHAPTER EIGHT

"Look! TV cameras!" Amelia pointed at
the crew filming outside the post office,
as she and Sam walked to Brambledown
Hall. It was Sunday morning at last,
and the whole village was buzzing with
excitement about the launch of the
gardening contest.

"They've cut the hedge into the shape
of a poodle!" cried Sam. Amelia laughed
as one of the postmen stood in front of it
for the cameras, pretending to tug a large
letter from the hedge-dog's mouth.

Mac yapped excitedly, dragging
Sam on to the next garden along. Sam
frowned at the wonky-shaped hedge in
the middle of the lawn. "Is it a rabbit…

or a squirrel?" He grinned. "They've done a really cool flower display, though – look, it's a rainbow!"

As they carried on up the road, every garden they passed had someone hard at work, trimming hedges and finishing off flower displays.

When they eventually reached the driveway leading up to Brambledown

Hall, Sam kept a tight grip on Mac's lead. Amelia knew he didn't want to take any chances with the deer.

"I hope our deer got back safely," Amelia said, as they walked towards the big house.

"It sounds like it ran in the right direction," Sam reassured her. "I'm sure it found its way back to the herd."

They stepped inside Brambledown Hall and Amelia gasped as she looked around. It was even busier than when they'd first come, with plants everywhere and TV people running around with clipboards and cameras.

Sam nudged her. "Look, it's our

celebrity guest!" Bernard Bloom was
sitting in the far corner with his head
tilted back, as a makeup artist powdered
his nose. He was wearing a green suit
with a purple flower pattern. Pansy
perched on a stool beside him, as an
assistant dressed her in a dog coat
made of the same flowery material as
Bernard's suit.

Amelia's heart leapt. "This might be my last chance to get Bernard Bloom's autograph before he gets too busy with the show!" She made her way over, pulling out the notebook and pen Gran had given her, as she waited for the makeup artist to finish.

Eventually, Mr Bloom straightened up and wrinkled his nose, as though he was trying not to sneeze.

"Excuse me, Mr Bloom, can I please get your autograph for my gran?" Amelia asked him. "She's a huge fan!"

"Of course!" Mr Bloom took the notebook, scrawled his name across the page and added a little flower

beneath. "Is your gran entering any of the contests? I can't be seen to have favourites!" He winked.

Amelia shook her head. "My mum was going to enter some roses, but they got eaten by a deer."

Bernard's eyes widened. "I heard about that! It's actually given me a really good idea for a slot on my show: How to deer-proof your garden!"

A man wearing large headphones around his neck came towards them, so Amelia thanked Mr Bloom and headed over to Kasia. She held on to Blossom's lead tightly as Sam came towards her, dragged along by an eager Mac.

"Did it work?" Amelia asked Kasia, breathlessly. "Did Blossom sleep through the night?"

Kasia nodded enthusiastically. "Yes, thank goodness! I'm so grateful to you both! I actually brought the washing basket here with me today." She pointed at a suit of armour, and Amelia spotted the blue basket sticking out from behind it. "Would you mind settling Blossom into it for me? I think she's starting to get a bit overwhelmed by all the noise."

"No problem!" Amelia grinned and took hold of Blossom's lead. She led Blossom over to the basket and rearranged the blankets to make them nice and snuggly. She placed some toys inside while Sam draped one end of a blanket over the suit of armour's shield, and the other end over a nearby chair.

Blossom jumped inside and curled up straight away. Mac sniffed at the den and looked up at Sam, confused.

"You don't need a den, Mac!" Sam said, laughing. "You'll sleep anywhere!"

Amelia stood up, letting the blanket fall

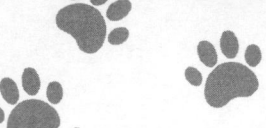

over the basket. "It's funny how animals can have such different personalities – even ones from the same species!"

They left Blossom to rest and wandered over to the window. Amelia leaned her elbows on the windowsill and gazed into the distance, trying to spot the deer.

Just then, a bell rang and a woman holding a clapperboard called out: "Silence on set! Filming is about to begin!" She snapped the two halves of the board together and Bernard Bloom stepped in front of the cameras.

"Welcome to a very special edition of *Blooming Brilliant!*" Bernard announced. "We're coming to you today from

the village of Welford. I now declare
the annual gardening show …" He
brandished a pair of pruning scissors and
aimed them at a red ribbon tied between
a pair of pot plants. "Open!" He snipped
the ribbon in two and everyone cheered.

A movement outside caught Amelia's

eye and she glanced out the window again. The deer herd was racing across the grass in the far distance.

She squinted. They were too far away to see properly, but she hoped her deer was with them.

As the hall fell silent again, waiting for Bernard to continue, she heard a little snore coming from the laundry basket and grinned. *We did it!* Blossom looked snug and happy in her den. *I don't think we need to worry about her barking at night any more,* Amelia thought happily. *We might not have saved Mum's roses from the deer, but at least we helped one little Blossom.*

The End

Turn over for a sneak peek at
Amelia and Sam's next adventure!

ANIMAL ARK

Owl All Alone

Lucy Daniels

Amelia stood up and pushed her hair back from her face. She felt hot and sweaty from digging in the morning sun, and her arms ached, but she let out a contented sigh. "Do you think this will be deep enough?" she asked.

Her friend Izzy stood nearby, holding a lavender plant. Clusters of little purple petals seemed to explode out from the green stems. "I think so," Izzy said.

Amelia stood back, letting the breeze cool her skin while Izzy planted the lavender into the hole.

"Good job!" said Miss Hafiz, Amelia's teacher. She was returning from the water butt with an overflowing watering can. "This garden's really taking shape!"

Amelia smiled as she gazed around the school's small plot. Leaves and twigs littered the grass from a storm the night before. But even so, the place looked transformed. Amelia and her classmates had cleared the weeds from around patches of geraniums and peonies, and fragrant flowers and shrubs now filled the newly dug beds.

"What a good idea it was to create a wildlife garden, Amelia," Miss Hafiz said. "And it's kind of you both to give up some of your half-term to come and finish the work."

A warm glow of pride spread through

Amelia. "I can't wait until it's finished!" she said. "We should get all sorts of birds and insects."

"I never really thought of gardening before," Izzy said. Her cheeks were flushed as she got to her feet. "But with the whole village working on their gardens for the Welford Gardening Competition, it's like the latest craze!"

"Especially this year," Miss Hafiz said, "with all the buzz the TV show is creating. You can hardly go outdoors without bumping into a camera crew filming someone's flowerbeds!"

Excitement bubbled inside Amelia as she thought of the show. "I can't believe they're going to dedicate a whole episode of *Blooming Brilliant* to the gardening competition!"

Izzy giggled. "Although it's kind of scary too. I keep thinking I'll walk past a camera without noticing and end up on telly wearing some goofy expression."

"Well, you're safe in here," Miss Hafiz said. "Look – the bees have already found your lavender!" She pointed towards a pair of honey bees buzzing around the purple flowers. "How about we rake up the leaves from the storm last night?"

Amelia checked her watch. "Uh-oh!" she said. "I'm supposed to be meeting

Sam up at Brambledown Hall.
We promised Kasia we'd help set up
for filming."

"Don't worry – Izzy and I will finish
up here," Miss Hafiz said. "You've done
so much already, Amelia!"

When Amelia reached Brambledown
Hall, she found the long, sweeping
driveway full of cars. People hurried
about pushing large black cases on
trolleys across the gravel. *Film equipment*,
guessed Amelia. *The crew are setting up!*

The heavy wooden doors to
Brambledown stood open. Inside the

entrance hall, more darkly clad film technicians were busy running cables over the black and white tiles. Amelia heard the low hum of voices coming from the ballroom and carefully picked her way over the cables and down a corridor.

In the ballroom, she found engineers rigging cameras in front of long tables covered with pots of flowers and shrubs. Sam was busy lifting more pots from a cart and adding them to the display.

"I was starting to think you weren't coming!" Sam said, grinning as Amelia joined him.

**Read Owl All Alone
to find out what happens next ...**

Animal Advice

Do you love animals as much as Amelia and Sam? Here are some tips on how to look after them from veterinary surgeon Sarah McGurk.

Caring for your pet

1. Animals need clean water at all times.
2. They need to be fed too – ask your vet what kind of food is best, and how much the animal needs.
3. Some animals, such as dogs, need exercise every day.
4. Animals also need lots of love. You should always be very gentle with your pets and be careful not to do anything that might hurt them.

When to go to the vet

Sometimes animals get ill. Like you, they will mostly get better on their own. But if your pet has hurt itself or seems very unwell, then a trip to the vet might be needed. Some pets also need to be vaccinated, to prevent them from getting dangerous diseases. Your vet can tell you what your pet needs.

Helping wildlife

1. Always ask an adult before you go near any animals you don't know.

2. If you find an animal or bird which is injured or can't move, it is best not to touch it.

3. If you are worried, you can phone an animal charity such as the RSPCA (SSPCA in Scotland) for help.

Where animals need you!